Emmy
the Exaggerating
Elephant

Fenton
the Fearful Frog

Gertie
the Grungy Goat

Herbie
the Happy
Hamster

Ivy
the Impatient
Iguana

Ollie
the Obedient
Ostrich

Perry
the Polite
Porcupine

Queenie
the Quiet Quail

Rupert
the Resourceful
Rhinoceros

Wendy
the Wise
Woodchuck

Xavier
the X-ploring
Xenops

Yori
the Yucky Yak

Ziggy
the Zippy Zebra

Note To Parents

Gertie's Great Gifts
A story about neatness

In this story, Gertie the Grungy Goat wins a truckload of wonderful gifts including grooming and cleaning supplies. In preparation for an interview with a reporter from the local newspaper, Gertie's AlphaPet friends have fun showing her how she can use some of her gifts to improve her appearance and tidy her home. Gertie not only learns to clean, but she looks gorgeous, too.

In addition to enjoying this funny story with your child, you can use it to teach a gentle lesson about the important value of neatness and cleanliness.

You can also use this story to introduce the letter **G**. As you read about Gertie the Grungy Goat, ask your child to listen for all the words that start with **G** and point to the objects that begin with **G**. When you've finished reading the story, your child will enjoy doing the activity at the end of the book.

The AlphaPets™ characters were conceived and created by Ruth Lerner Perle.
Characters interpreted and designed by Deborah Colvin Borgo.
Cover design by the Antler & Baldwin Design Group.
Book design and production by Publishers' Graphics, Inc.
Logo design by Deborah Colvin Borgo and Nancy S. Norton.

Printed and Manufactured in the United States of America

Gertie's Great Gifts

RUTH LERNER PERLE

Illustrated by Richard Max Kolding

Grolier Enterprises Inc.   Danbury, Connecticut

Early one morning, Gertie the Grungy Goat was sitting on her sofa listening to her favorite radio program.

"And now, listeners," said Vinnie the Vocal Vulture, "it's time to play *Guess That Tune*! If I call you and you can guess the mystery tune I'm playing, the gong will sound and you will win a truckload of great gifts. So listen-up folks, and stay near your phone."

Gertie listened as Vinnie played the mystery tune.

"Ooh! I know that song!" cried Gertie, clapping her hands. "How I wish Vinnie would call me!"

Rring, Rring, Rrring! It was Gertie's telephone.

She pulled the phone out from under her sofa, and wiped the peanut butter off the receiver.

"Hello there, Gertie!" said a happy voice. "This is Vinnie from the *Guess That Tune* Show. You have thirty seconds to guess the tune we're playing. If you are correct, you'll win our grand prize! Go, go, Gertie."

"I know it! I know it!" cried Gertie. "The name of that tune is 'Goodbye Gorilla!'"

BONG! "Golly, gee," shouted Vinnie. "That's the gong! 'Goodbye Gorilla', it is! Good for you, Gertie! You've just won the grand prize, and all your gifts will be delivered today!"

Later that morning a big delivery truck arrived at Gertie's house.

Gertie's AlphaPet neighbors couldn't believe their eyes. One by one they came running over to help carry all the packages into the house.

The AlphaPets watched as Gertie opened her gifts.
The first box was full of bottles of shampoo, bubble
bath, soap, and toothpaste.

"Who needs all this goofy stuff!" said Gertie.

Next, Gertie unzipped a long garment bag. There was a green gown with matching shoes and golden gloves. And there was a hat with gigantic grapes all over it.

"Ooohh!" exclaimed Emmy the Exaggerating Elephant. "That's the most gorgeous gown I have ever, ever seen. And that hat — it's too, too divine. Just look at those green grapes! They look real!"

"I wish they *were* real," said Gertie, opening another box. "Then we could at least eat them."

Everyone was busy looking at the gifts when the doorbell rang. A messenger was there with a special delivery letter for Gertie. Gertie opened the envelope and smiled a great big smile.

"Oh, goody, goody, goody!" she shouted. "This is better than all these goofy gifts."

"What is it?" asked Bradley the Brave Bear.

"What is it?" asked Monty the Mimicking Mouse.

"It's a letter from the *AlphaPet Globe Gazette*," cried Gertie. "A news reporter is coming here this afternoon to interview me. My picture will be in the newspaper!"

Katy the Kind Koala looked around the room.

"Well, now," she said. "What a wonderful opportunity this is for us all. We can help Gertie get ready for her interview, and we can use some of these gifts to do it."

"Yes, yes," agreed Herbie the Happy Hamster. "That will be fun!"

"What do you mean, *get ready* for the interview? I *am* ready," said Gertie.

"Just wait," said Wendy the Wise Woodchuck. "You'll see that these are not such goofy gifts after all."

Wendy took Gertie's hand and said, "Some of us will go upstairs and help Gertie get ready, and the rest of you can clean up the living room. That way we'll be ready when the reporter comes."

"Get set for the greatest makeover ever!" whooped Emmy, and she ran up the stairs.

As soon as they were upstairs, the AlphaPets

rubbed and scrubbed,
washed and wiped,

rinsed and dried,

brushed and flossed,

combed and curled,
and clipped and filed.

"And now for the gown!" cried Emmy. "Oh yes! It's time for the gown. The glorious gown, the glittering gown, the shimmering, glimmering marvelous gown!

While Gertie was dressing, the rest of the AlphaPets were busy in the living room. They

washed and wiped,

swept and sponged,

sprayed and waxed,

buffed and puffed,

mopped and polished,

and cleared away the trash.

When Gertie was all ready, she looked in the mirror.

"Oh my goodness gracious! Is that really me?" she gasped.

Then Gertie went downstairs. Everything was shiny neat and squeaky clean.

"My goodness gracious," said Gertie. "My house is *sooooo* beautiful."

"You see," said Perry, "it's all thanks to those great gifts you got!"

"— and to my good AlphaPet friends," said Gertie.

When the *Globe* reporter came, she took pictures of Gertie and wrote the story of how Gertie had won all the great gifts on the *Guess That Tune!* program.

"Your picture will be on the front page of the evening paper," the reporter said. She thanked Gertie for her time, took her camera and notebook and rushed off.

Early that evening, while Gertie was admiring her sparkling house, she heard loud noises in the yard. Gertie looked out and saw crowds and crowds of AlphaPets waving newspapers and shouting "CONGRATULATIONS GERTIE! We came to celebrate with you!"

Everyone came running into Gertie's living room carrying their newspapers along with food and party games. They danced and ate and played for hours.

When the AlphaPets finally left, Gertie looked around her house. There were newspapers, cups, and cookie crumbs everywhere.

"My goodness gracious me! Look at this mess!"
sighed Gertie as she went to get the soap and mop and
vacuum cleaner.

"It's a good thing I got those goofy . . . I mean *great*
gifts! I'll have this place gleaming in no time."

These are the neatest words around.
Please remember them with me.

grapes

garden

gown

globe

guitar

gum

gift

gate

gloves

green

Look back at the pictures in the book, and try to find these and other things that begin with the letter G.

Know Your Alphabet

Aa Bb

Gg Hh

Mm Nn Oo Pp

Uu Vv Ww